AF505099

TRUST IS BUILT WITH CONSISTENCY

TRUST IS THE GLUE OF LIFE. IT'S THE MOST ESSENTIAL INGREDIENT IN EFFECTIVE COMMUNICATION. IT'S THE FOUNDATIONAL PRINCIPLE THAT HOLDS ALL RELATIONSHIPS.

SUPARNA GANGULY

Copyright © Suparna Ganguly
All Rights Reserved.

ISBN 979-888629130-8

This book has been published with all efforts taken to make the material error-free after the consent of the author. However, the author and the publisher do not assume and hereby disclaim any liability to any party for any loss, damage, or disruption caused by errors or omissions, whether such errors or omissions result from negligence, accident, or any other cause.

While every effort has been made to avoid any mistake or omission, this publication is being sold on the condition and understanding that neither the author nor the publishers or printers would be liable in any manner to any person by reason of any mistake or omission in this publication or for any action taken or omitted to be taken or advice rendered or accepted on the basis of this work. For any defect in printing or binding the publishers will be liable only to replace the defective copy by another copy of this work then available.

Augustine lived with his 36 adopted kids.

They loved to be with them.

Their happiness made him happy , their sadness made him sad .

He invasted all his time, emptions everything to them.

As He had no one of his own in his life, for whom he gave place to 36 Kids in his house.
Lucy was the youngest of them all,

she was 6 years old.

Augustine himself was 56 years old.
Despite his age,

he was mentally and physically much stronger .

30 years ago he lost all the happiness of his life and

then he found happiness through the kids.

Augustine himself was the only heir of a very rich

and established family.

His father was a reknowned business person .

After his parents' death,

all the property goes to him.
He loved everyone and helped the poor.

After his parents' demise,

he enrolled in the city's Famous College to study sociology,

where he met Jennifer.
Very beautiful woman full of life,

anyone who sees her will fall in love with her.
Augustine rarely spoke to anyone,

he looked at Jennifer but could not say anything.
Augustine's closest friend is Austin,

who is always with him, support him in his every move.

Growing up together, Augustine and Austin know each other a lot.

Austine also a person with full of life ,

always cracking jokes , doing fun.

He was completly opposite to Augustine despite this , they were best friends .

Augustin only share his feelings with him , and Austin always stay by his side .

Austin and Jennifer were alike.

After a brief acquaintance,

Jennifer and Austin became very good friends.

Austin knew Augustine's feelings towards her,

so without delay,

befriended Augustine and Jennifer.

But Augustine is too embarrassed to talk to Jennifer.

One day they decide to go for a trip .

They plan a two-days vacation.

Actually this planned created by Austin.

So they left for their vacation,

they enjoyed a lot ,

There, in a state of intoxication,

Augustine tells Jennifer what is on his mind, and proposed her.

Jennifer leaves without saying a word.
When they get home,

Jennifer stopped responding his calls.

they go to college after a week.

Augustin himself a very shy person he thought may be Jennifer was not feel good after knowing his emptions,

so he thought to say sorry to her.

Augustive with his all collective efforts said her : Sorry Jennifer.

Jennifer first ignored him .

Then hearing this Jennifer laughs and
says: Idiot,I love you too.
Every Girl Wants Someone Like You, Augustine.

(Jennifer liked him as well as Augustine was a very calm and compose person,
Augustin a perfect guy a girl can desire . Handsome, wealthy, compose,
understanding , everything attracked Jennifer towards him)

They kissed each other.

Austin was happiest to see Augustine and Jennifer together.

Their relationship started within 1 month,

Jennifer proposed for marriage to Augustine.

Augustine agrees with her without wasting any time.

Within a few days, Augustine and Jennifer were married.

After marriage, they started living a very beautiful life.

Austin also used to visit thier place frequently.

After few days They decided they will do their own business,

Augustine wanted to open NGO,

so he does not agree to the business,

but Jennifer and Austin repeatedly approch him so agrees to do business together.

In the meantime,

Austin informed them he is going to marry a woman named Nancy . Austin says yes to the marriage

because his parents fixed everything ,

he dont even know her.

Nancy and Austin are married within 2months. Nancy

was a very quiet girl who liked to talk less.

Jennifer and Augustine invite Nancy and Austin after their marriage for dinner. In fact,

Jennifer and Augustine understand that their relationship is not good,

there is only emphasis. After they leave,

Augustine tells Jennfer that they need time to adjust ,

they dont know each other hence this situation created.

After few days Jennifer finds out that she is third month pregnant. Augustine is very happy to know. Finally they became parents.

Augustine plans to have a big celebration for her 6-month-old daughter.

Austin's commute increased.
Augustine is an ordinary man,

down to earth.
He did not want to complicate things.

The day of the party comes and Austin stays at Augustin's house the day before.

Augustine says: Why didn't you bring Nancy?

Before saying anything Austin,
Jennifer said: What will she do here ?

she cant even enjoy properly.

She will get bored, better she come tomorrow people will be there she will like the atmosphere.

Nancy comes to the party in the evening,
And

continue to follow Augustine's movement,

Augustine notices that,

Augustine personally asks

Nancy: Do you want to say something?

Nancy replied: See you after the celebration near to pool area .

After the party, Augustine went to see Nancy.

realizing the opportunity,

Nancy showed Augustine some pictures which made Augustine puzzled.

He got amazed to see those pictures for a while.

The pictures were of Jennifer,

Jennifer's picture was kept in Austin room.

There was even a picture of Jennifer taking a bath,

Augustine was very surprised to see that he remained silent.

Nancy said in a tearful voice: "Jennifer and Austin have an illicit affair that they call friendship."

Augustine was still silent.

Nancy says she thinks of Baby Jennifer and Austin,

Can't hear this, Augustine slaps Nancy and left that place.

Then Augustine start follows their movement,

Seeing their closeness he also start thinking their affir was true.

Two days after Augustine and Jennifer's anniversary,

Jennifer plans to surprise Augustine,

Jennifer takes her baby for visit her parents home,

and says she's going to see her parents.

Augustine says: Is it really important to go now ? after 2 days our anniversary we can go together after anniversary.

Jennifer says: No, I need to go mom's health also detoriate few days ago.

2 days later,

on the morning of the anniversary,

Augustine's mind was not obeying it,

everything was spinning in his head.

He received a call in the morning ,

A man on the phone says in a hoarse voice: Am I talking to Augustine?

Augustine says: Yes, who are you?

unknown person says: there was an accident on St.Louis Road,

your wife was in the car .

We just see the id hence contacting you.

Augustine cries and says: My baby was in the car, is she fine?

He replied: No, they are not there,you need to be at the hospital to identify the bodies.

Augustine rushed towards hospital and

saw that there were 3 people in the accident, the third person was Austin.

After a while Nancy comes,

Nancy looks at 3 people and says: Now I had no doubt I was right.

Augustine wiped her eyes and left.

Then he changed everything in his life and

adopted childrens and decide to give them a beautiful life by adopting them.

After Austin died,

Nancy married another man and had a good life.

After leaving Austin,

Nancy received ownership of the Austin property.

Nancy was leading a beautiful life with her son and husband,

suddenly she found
Austin's diary, where Austin

posted beautiful pictures of her and Augustine's friendship,

she start read the dairy.

Shee found out later in Dairy that he had fallen in love with Jennifer

after seeing her for the first time.

Suddenly her baby start crying while reading.

It's been 2 days and one night she can't sleep,

so she decided to read more.
On that day, she found out that

Austin's love was became an obsession for Jeniiffer.

Austin called Jeniffer in her anniversary day and he preplanned it , he was aware that she goes to her parents,

Jennifer doesn't know Austin's intension,

so when he received call from Austin she agreed to meet him.

Austin called her to express his feelings towards her,

but they did not return.

It was planned by Austin to meet her on that day,

but what was happened after that day nobdy know.

but Nancy realized that Jennifer was not at fault.

Nancy decides she will tell Augustine without delay.

After a long time Nancy visited Augustine place,

But Augustine was not happy to see Nancy after so long.

Augustine said: Nancy? What brought you here?

Nancy said: There are some things left to tell you, so I'm coming here.

Augustine: Is there anything left for you to do after so many years?

Nancy: If I had said no, it would not have been possible for me to spend the
rest of my life.

Augustine: What are you talking about?

Nancy: I got this diary from Austin for which I came here.

Austin and Jennifer had no relationship,

Austin liked Jennifer from day one,

Jennifer didn't even know Austin's feelings, we were wrong.

Augustine listened to everything and watched Dairy silently but not very attentively.

After hearing all this,

Augustine just said: Nancy, want to Eat something?

Nancy: What ? are you not feel sad about it ? Knowing that there is no fault of the person who has been thinking badly for so long?

Augustine was still silent,

Lucy ran to Augustine and he hugged Lucy.

Augustine said : I thought she was wrong,

I got punishment for that ,

i lost my child i lost my wife whom i love most.

now my life is in their name only see this childs, and he left.
Nancy looked up in surprise.

Everyone says that if we don't see something with own eyes,

we shouldnt believe,

but the truth is even if we see with our eyes,

we see wrong, we think wrong, everything comes because of our wrong thinking.

Trusting someone is very important.

If there is trust there is love , if you cant trust a person you cant love .

Augustine learn his lession but its late for him .

He lost his everything then he realised .

Story written by :

Suparna Ganguly.

Contents

www.ingramcontent.com/pod-product-compliance
Lightning Source LLC
Chambersburg PA
CBHW072133150726

48002CB00007B/2692